MINECRAFT
STONESWORD SAGA

MOBS RULE!

© 2022 Mojang AB. All Rights Reserved. Minecraft, the Minecraft logo and the Mojang Studios logo are trademarks of the Microsoft group of companies.

Published in the United States by Random House Children's Books, a division of Penguin Random House LLC, 1745 Broadway, New York, NY 10019, and in Canada by Penguin Random House Canada Limited, Toronto. Random House and the colophon are registered trademarks of Penguin Random House LLC.

rhcbooks.com
minecraft.net

Library of Congress Cataloging-in-Publication Data is available upon request.
ISBN 978-1-9848-5075-1 (trade)
ISBN 978-1-9848-5076-8 (library binding)—ISBN 978-1-9848-5077-5 (ebook)

Cover design by Diane Choi

Printed in the United States of America
10 9 8 7 6 5 4 3

MOBS RULE!

By Nick Eliopulos
Illustrated by Alan Batson and Chris Hill

Random House 🏠 New York

MORGAN

ASH

HARPER

LAYERS!

PO

JODI

THEO

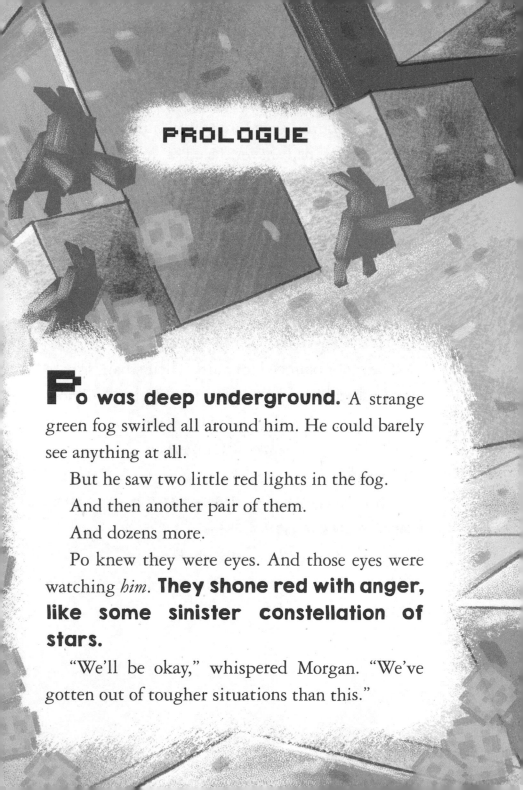

PROLOGUE

Po was deep underground. A strange green fog swirled all around him. He could barely see anything at all.

But he saw two little red lights in the fog.

And then another pair of them.

And dozens more.

Po knew they were eyes. And those eyes were watching *him*. **They shone red with anger, like some sinister constellation of stars.**

"We'll be okay," whispered Morgan. "We've gotten out of tougher situations than this."

But Po wasn't so sure.

They'd never seen anything quite like this before. They had never faced a mighty *swarm* of angry, vicious Minecraft mobs all working together as if they shared a single brain. A *hive mind* controlled these mobs, and its instructions were simple: **Destroy Po and his friends.**

It was hard not to be worried. Even if the mobs *were* awfully cute.

"Here they come," warned Morgan.

The mobs bounced forward. Their small, square eyes flashed like rubies in the torchlight. And now Po could see what they were up against.

It was a *tidal wave* of dangerous . . . *adorable* **bunnies**.

"Run away!" cried Po. **"RUN AWAY, RUN AWAY, RUN AWAY!"**

But his friends were already fleeing.

And the rabbits were gaining with each passing second.

Chapter 1

WHEN THINGS SPLIT APART, WHOSE FAULT IS IT ANYWAY?

Po Chen tried his best to ignore the strange hole in the Minecraft sky.

His friends had recently started calling it **the Fault.** Though it was small, it was easy to see in the daytime. Against the light blue color of the sky, the blacked-out pixels were hard to miss.

But Minecraft was Po's happy place. He was not going to stress out over a little thing like a hole in the sky. Strange and wonderful things happened here all the time. Why worry about it?

"Well, *I'm* worried," said Po's friend Morgan Mercado. Morgan was a Minecraft expert, and he didn't like it when the game acted unpredictably.

"I'D LIKE TO GET A CLOSER LOOK AT IT," said Harper Houston. While Morgan tended to react to situations quickly, Harper liked to gather facts before coming to conclusions.

"If we want answers, the best place to find them is in the game's code," said Theo Grayson. Everyone shot him a look. His would-be programming and modding skills had gotten them into trouble before. Theo shrugged and added sheepishly, "It's just a suggestion."

"WHATEVER THE FAULT IS . . . it's definitely not cute," said Jodi Mercado. She was Morgan's little sister, and she enjoyed meeting cute animal mobs and adding artistic flair to the things they built. **Wild adventures, epic mob battles, and eerie holes in the sky**

were not her idea of a great Minecraft session.

"La la la," said Po, putting his blocky hands to his ears. "Can't hear you."

Morgan scowled. "Be serious, Po," he said. "Aren't you even a little bit curious about what the Fault is? Or about what caused it?"

"OF COURSE I'M CURIOUS," said Po. "But just because it's *weird* doesn't mean it's a problem. I mean, this version of Minccraft has always been weird."

Po knew Morgan was making a good point. After all, he and his friends weren't just playing Minecraft—they were *living* it. Thanks to their science teacher's experimental VR technology, they were able to visit a digital landscape that looked and acted almost exactly like their favorite game. *Almost* exactly. There were occasional exceptions . . . like the artificial intelligence named the Evoker King who called this place home.

But the Evoker King had turned out to be a pretty cool guy. So maybe the black spot in the blue sky would turn out to

be pretty cool, too?

They had been walking across the Overworld for days, stopping occasionally to gather resources or fight a zombie or chase a chicken around just for fun. It To outsiders it might have looked like aimless wandering, but the kids were on a mission.

They were hunting butterflies.

Butterflies—like Faults and artificial intelligences—didn't belong in a normal game of Minecraft. The small, colorful mobs had only appeared recently, and they had something to do with the Evoker

King's dramatic transformation.

"I saw one!" said Theo. He peered into the distance. "I can't see it anymore. BUT IT WENT THAT WAY."

Po looked in the direction Theo was pointing. Across the plain, there was a mountain, and at the base of that mountain, he saw a small collection of homes. "Hey, there's a village over there."

"We might as well check it out," said Harper. "MAYBE WE CAN PICK UP SOME SUPPLIES . . . OR SOME CLUES."

Po agreed. He hoped they were on the right track, and that they would soon find a way to help the Evoker King. Shortly after the kids had become friends with the Evoker King, their AI ally had turned to stone—or so it had appeared. It was more accurate to say that the Evoker King had been *cocooned* in stone. And when that cocoon had split open, several mysterious mobs had emerged. **Those mysterious mobs were all made from pieces of the Evoker King's programming.** If they wanted to put their friend back together, they needed to find each piece. And the unusual digital butterflies that had appeared when the cocoon first split open seemed to appear near those mysterious mobs. It was almost like the game was leaving a path for the kids to follow.

And right now, that path was leading them to a village.

The village was a small one, with only a few houses. Its residents were all going about their usual business.

"See?" said Po. "They're not worried about the Fault, either." **He chuckled, remembering that he was using an alien skin for his**

avatar today. "Hey, Earthling," he said to the nearest villager. "Take us to your leader!"

The villager only honked in reply and kept walking.

Theo frowned. "I was actually *hoping* there'd be something unusual about this place," he said. "I don't think we're going to find the next piece of the Evoker King in a normal village."

A farmer held out an emerald for Harper to see. "Oh!" said Harper. **"THE FARMER WANTS TO TRADE AN EMERALD FOR SOME HAY THAT'S IN MY INVENTORY. I think we can spare it. . . ."**

"Hey, look over there!" said Jodi. She pointed up

the nearby extreme hills biome and the mountain that loomed over the village.

"What is it?" asked Morgan. "Another butterfly?"

"Even better," said Jodi. **"IT'S A LLAMA!"**

"Wow," said Po. "Good eyes, Jodi." The llama was some distance away. It looked tiny! But now that Jodi had pointed it out, Po could see it walking around about halfway up the mountain.

"I haven't seen a llama in *weeks*," said Jodi. "Can we go visit? **I WANT TO PET IT!"**

Morgan shook his head. "We need to focus on the mission," he said.

"Aw, come on, Morgan," said Po. "I want to help the Evoker King as much as you do, but this village is a dead end. I don't see any butterflies."

He shrugged. "And llamas *are* pretty cute."

"Besides," added Harper, **"CLIMBING THE MOUNTAIN MIGHT BE A GOOD STRATEGY.** We'll be able to see for miles in every direction. Maybe that will help us figure out where to go next."

"Yeah, okay," said Morgan. "That makes sense." **Jodi gave Po a fist bump** and a smile.

The mountain was tall, but it wasn't too steep. Po and the others were able to take it one block at a time. And in Minecraft, they didn't have to worry about altitude sickness or landslides or any of the other dangers of real-life mountain climbing.

They did have to worry about falling, though. **Falling from such a great height was as dangerous in Minecraft as it was in real life.**

Po decided not to look down.

But when he looked up, he saw the Fault, too close to ignore.

By the time they reached the llama, the sun was getting lower. It dipped behind the mountain, casting everything on their side in shadow.

"Be careful," said Morgan. "Even though it's daytime . . . monsters can spawn in the shadows."

"HOW CAN YOU THINK OF MONSTERS AT A TIME LIKE THIS?" said Jodi, and she held out her blocky hands toward the llama. It was facing away from them and hadn't noticed them yet. "Hello, my precious! What's your name?"

"Hm," said Po, deciding to guess the llama's name. "I think it looks like a *Winifred*."

Jodi chuckled, and she placed a hand on the llama's back. **The animal spun around to look at her and its eyes shone red.**

There was something sinister and unnatural about those red eyes.

"Okay," said Po. "Definitely not Winifred!"

Jodi just had time to gasp before the llama spat at her. She flashed red as she took damage from the projectile spit. She was also knocked back—dangerously close to the edge.

"CAREFUL!" said Morgan, and he quickly

pulled his sister to his side.

"I don't understand," she said. "Why did it attack me?"

"It's *still* attacking," warned Theo. **"LOOK OUT!"**

Theo was right. The llama appeared to be furious. It reared up and kicked at them, spitting again, and all the while, it bleated angrily.

Po pulled a sword from his inventory, but he hesitated. "I don't really want to hurt it!" he said.

"THEN GET AWAY FROM IT!" said Morgan. "Everybody, retreat!"

Po didn't need to be told twice. He put his

sword away and followed the others as they fled the angry animal.

A glob of spit passed by his head, narrowly missing him. Bleating sounded from just behind him. The llama was actually *chasing* them.

"This is too weird!" Theo cried.

Harper was in the lead, and as she headed down the mountain, she curved around it to the other side. "This way!" she said. "We have to get out of its view."

PO FOLLOWED. As he rounded the bend, he saw a small fissure in the ground, just past the foot of the mountain. It looked like an earthquake had left a narrow crack right in the grassy dirt of the

plains. Harper ran into the fissure, followed by the others.

Po was the last one to enter. The others all stood with their backs pressed against the stone wall, hiding in the dark. He joined them.

There were sounds of bleating from outside, and shuffling hooves. But the llama didn't follow them inside.

"I think we lost it," whispered Harper.

"WHY WAS IT SO AGGRESSIVE?" asked Jodi. "Did I do something wrong?"

Po turned to Morgan, expecting him to have something to say about what was normal and abnormal llama behavior. But Morgan had stepped

a little farther into the fissure. **He looked astonished.**

"Check it out, everybody," he said. "It's a lush cave biome."

Po joined Morgan and peered deeper into the cave. He was surprised to see so much color beneath the stone-gray mountain. He saw green moss, pink flowers, brown roots, and bright blue water.

"I've never seen this biome before," said Theo.

"Me neither," said Harper. **"I'D LIKE TO EXPLORE IT!"**

"It's better than going back out *there*," said Jodi, hugging herself.

"Let's set up our beds," said Morgan. "This is as good a spot as any. Tomorrow, we can take our time exploring the cave."

It sounded like a good plan to Po. He had homework waiting for him back in the real world . . . **and something else on his mind, as well.**

Soon, Woodsword Middle School would be holding an election.

And Po didn't intend to miss out on that.

Chapter 2

A SPOONFUL OF COMPETITION NEVER HURT ANYBODY—BUT A FORKFUL OF BAD IDEAS WILL POKE YOU IN THE EYE EVERY TIME!

The next day at school, Jodi was still thinking about the llama.

"You should have seen it, **Baron Sweetcheeks**," she said to the class hamster. "It was the *meanest* llama of all time. **Eight feet tall ... with red eyes, and fangs ...**"

Baron Sweetcheeks trembled in her hands. At first, she worried that she had frightened the hamster. But then she realized he was just excited to be surrounded by so much food. (It was lunchtime, and Jodi had brought him to the cafeteria.)

"You're exaggerating," said Theo. **"The llama did not have fangs."**

"She's right about the eyes,
though," said Harper. "They were
as red as rubies."

Morgan was clearly troubled. "I
don't know what it means," he said. "But I wonder
if it has something to do with the Evoker King.
And I also wonder . . . is it sanitary to have Baron
Sweetcheeks at our lunch table?"

Po gasped. "How dare you!" he said. "The
Baron is *immaculately* clean. He bathes more often
than you do!"

"And I *need* him here for emotional support,"
said Jodi, hugging the hamster close. "I see that
llama's mean old face every time I close my eyes!"

Harper shrugged. "To be honest, I'm glad he's
here, too," she said. "Because I've got bologna for

lunch, and there's no way I can eat it all."

"Ooh," said Theo. **"I love bologna."**

"Well, now I've heard everything," said Harper, and she handed him half her sandwich. **The hamster squeaked with envy.**

"I'm glad you could join us today, Baron Sweetcheeks," said Po, suddenly sounding gravely serious.

Jodi giggled. Po only sounded *gravely serious* when he was being silly.

"You're a hamster," Po continued, "but you're also part of our team. So it's only fitting that you're here for my big announcement. I, Po Chen . . . have decided to run for class president!"

Baron Sweetcheeks didn't seem especially impressed by this news. He was fixated on Theo's gelatin dessert. But everyone else around the table gave a little cheer.

"That's exciting news!" said Jodi.

"Totally," said Theo. **"YOU'VE GOT MY VOTE."**

"How can we help?" asked Harper.

Morgan scratched his chin. "Po . . . are you sure you have time for this?" he asked.

Jodi elbowed her brother.

"What?" he said. "Class president is a lot of responsibility! And Po has a lot going on, between schoolwork, basketball, drama club, and, you know . . ." He lowered his voice. **"Searching the Overworld for the missing fragments of a sentient artificial intelligence so that we can put him back together again."**

In response, Po waved around a homemade "Vote for Po" pennant. "It's fine," he said. "Drama club is on break for a little while. And as class president, I'll be able to set the schedule for the whole student government. **That means no** meetings on days we play Minecraft."

"All right then," said Morgan, and he smiled. "I'm in. And I'm impressed. I heard you have to fill out a *lot* of paperwork to get your name on the ballot. I don't know when you had time to do that."

"Paperwork, you say?" Po gulped. "Sounds like . . . I should get on that."

"Po!" said Harper. **"That paperwork is due this week!"**

"Well, how was I supposed to know that?" asked Po.

"The student council mentioned it on the morning announcements," answered Theo. "Every morning. For the last three weeks."

Po just shrugged. "Maybe the paperwork can get done quickly if we all pitch in," he suggested.

Jodi reached across the table to pat him on the shoulder. **"We'll help you, Po,"** she said. "Don't worry. I've got a good feeling about—"

Before Jodi could finish her sentence, an amplified voice boomed across the cafeteria. "Good afternoon, fellow students!"

Everyone turned in their seats. At the front of

the room was a girl holding a megaphone. Jodi had never met her, but she recognized her outfit. The girl was wearing a Wildling Scout uniform similar to the one their friend Ash used to wear, and a sash full of merit badges.

"**I'm Shelly Silver**," said the girl. "And I'd like to announce my candidacy for president of student government!"

Everyone in the cafeteria applauded. Even Jodi felt it was the polite thing to do. But Po just glared and gripped his pennant tighter.

"**Thanks, everybody,**" said Shelly. "I have a small—but sweet—treat for you all today." Her smile flashed white, even at this distance. "So remember me when it's time to cast your ballot. **Vote for Shelly!**"

As soon as Shelly had finished speaking, a dozen Wildling Scouts emerged from the kitchen. They each carried a tray piled high with little ice cream cups, and they circulated through the cafeteria, giving each student a free ice cream and spoon.

Jodi felt a little guilty accepting the dessert. But she would have felt worse turning it down.

She could feel Po's eyes burning into her as she took her first bite. It was *really* good ice cream. But she tried not to show it.

"Check it out, Po," said Theo, and he held up the spoon he'd been given. "There are words printed on it."

Jodi looked at her own spoon. Theo was right. The spoons had a simple slogan: "Vote for Shelly."

"Looks like you've got some competition, buddy," said Morgan.

Po nodded grimly, his pennant drooping as if in defeat.

Chapter 3

THREE HINTS ABOUT WHAT'S IN THE WATER: IT'S AN AMPHIBIAN. IT'S A PASSIVE MOB. AND IT'S DIFFICULT TO SPELL!

Po wasn't happy to learn that Shelly Silver wanted to be class president, too. He had hoped to be the only person on the ballot. **Now he would have to plan a real campaign.** He had to convince everybody to vote for him . . . somehow.

He expected to be grumpy about it for the rest of the day. But that afternoon, when he and his friends reconnected to their shared Minecraft server, he forgot his irritation almost immediately. **The lush cave biome was just too awe-inspiring for his rotten mood to last.**

He had spent a lot of time underground. Usually that meant being surrounded by gray diorite, gray

andesite, gray deepslate . . . **and occasionally some bright-orange lava.**

But this cave had plants. Flowers! Faintly glowing berries grew upon long, hanging vines, and tree roots hung from the stony ceiling, like fingers reaching down for him.

"Should we take some of the roots with us?" asked Theo. **He had removed a pair of iron shears from his inventory.**

"Sure," said Harper. "Let's take a little of everything! You never know what we might be able to use later. Po, grab that flower!"

"On it," said Po, but before he had a chance, he heard Jodi call for him.

"Po!" squealed Jodi. "Harper! **COME HERE, QUICK! YOU'VE GOT TO SEE THIS!**"

Po and Harper shared a grin. Then they rushed

over to see what had made Jodi so excited.

"LOOK!" she said. **"IN THE WATER!"**

Po stepped right up to the edge of the underground lake. He bent over and peered into the water.

Nothing could have prepared him for the strange creature that peered back at him.

THERE IN THE WATER WAS A LONG, SKINNY ANIMAL WITH BRIGHT PINK COLORING. At first Po thought it must be a fish—maybe an eel—but that wasn't right. Unlike a fish, it had limbs. Its face almost reminded him of a puppy's.

Jodi gripped his arm. "It . . . it . . ." She took a steadying breath, then bellowed, *"It's even cuter than a llama!"*

Before Po could stop her, Jodi dove into the water. Luckily, the mob appeared to be friendly.

It swam right up to Jodi as if curious, and she chased it, laughing.

"WHAT'S THAT THING?" Po asked.

"It's an axolotl," answered Harper. "It's an amphibian—a type of salamander. Some people call it a 'walking fish' because, well, that's sort of what it looks like."

"I don't think I've seen an axolotl in Minecraft before," said Theo. He and Morgan had joined them at the edge of the water. "Are they safe to be around?"

"Sure," said Morgan. **"THEY'LL ATTACK SOME UNDERWATER MOBS,** but they're passive toward players. And fun fact: they can heal when they get damaged."

"Just like in real life!" said Harper. "Axolotls can regrow lost limbs—or even organs. They're like little miracles. Unfortunately, they're endangered. . . ."

As fascinating as all this was to hear Po found himself increasingly jealous of the good time Jodi was having. "Sorry, everybody," he said. "I've got to see it up close for myself!"

And he dove into the water.

There were two axolotls now, swimming in

circles around Jodi. One was pink, and one was gold.

Po joined the swimming, petting the axolotls when they got close. They were weirdly adorable, and Po wished he could just stay down there and never come up for air. All his problems were above the water's surface. Down here, it was a party.

But then he caught sight of Jodi. She looked worried—*panicked.* She was flapping her arms madly, trying to tell him

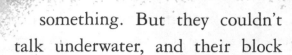

something. But they couldn't talk underwater, and their block hands made it difficult to communicate with gestures. What was she trying to warn him about?

THEN, SUDDENLY, PO WAS FALLING THROUGH OPEN AIR.

Oh, he thought. *Waterfall.* That was what she'd been trying to tell him.

That underground lake had been more of an underground *river,* and he'd been swept up in the current without even realizing it!

Po flipped head over rump, and before he had a chance to worry about where he would land, he splashed down into a *true* underground lake. He swam to the surface, but it was hard to see anything. **He was really deep underground now,** and except for the light of the glow berries high above him, it was dark.

"Po!" came Morgan's voice from above. "Are you okay?"

"Yeah!" Po shouted back. **"COME ON DOWN, YOU GUYS. THE WATER'S FINE!"**

He thought they might all dive into the lake,

but they took a safer route. He could see them clearly by the light of the torches Harper was leaving behind as they walked carefully down a rocky slope.

Once they reached the bottom, the whole cavern slowly revealed itself to Po, the light peeling away the darkness a little bit at a time. It was a huge subterranean space, with multiple lakes, a giant waterfall, and dozens of dark tunnel openings.

There was a splash nearby, and Po saw that the axolotls had followed him down the waterfall. The mobs twisted and turned playfully in the water.

"This is so cool," said Theo as he reached ground level. He and Jodi and Harper and Morgan all walked in different directions, poking their heads into side tunnels and **placing torches all around the cavern.**

Morgan stepped up to where Po was swimming. "I was worried when you went over the edge," he said.

"IT WAS A BIG DROP, but you didn't need to worry," said Po. "I've got luck on my side."

Morgan grinned—and then he noticed the green mist gathering at his feet.

"Uh," said Morgan, his smile dropping away. "What's *that* about?"

He looked around for answers. He looked left and right. Up and down.

But he didn't look behind him. **So he didn't see what Po saw.**

And what Po saw was a monster. It skittered out of the dark tunnel, right at Morgan's back.

Chapter 4

AXOLOTLS: SUPER CUTE! TERRIBLE JUDGES OF CHARACTER!

Morgan could tell by the look on Po's face that **something was terribly wrong.**

Po seemed to be warning him about something. Still floating in the underground lake, he opened and closed his mouth, looking like a fish, making no sound. Morgan had been playing Minecraft a long time, so experience quickly translated Po's expression: *Behind you!*

It was a cave spider.

But it was far larger than any cave spider Morgan had ever seen. Its eight legs were as thick as tree trunks. Its ten ruby-red eyes shone with eerie intelligence. Its fangs dripped with green venom.

And on its abdomen . . . **was the frightening image of a skull.**

Morgan didn't hesitate. He quickly swapped his torch for a weapon. He chose a diamond sword that had been enchanted with sharpness.

He had never fought a mob quite like this one. But no mob could survive for long against such a powerful sword.

Morgan leaped forward and slashed.

He was fast—but the spider was faster. It jumped back, much farther and higher than he expected. In an instant, it was up on the edge of a looming cliff, too far away to hit with a sword.

"Careful," said Theo. He was gripping his own sword as he came to stand beside Morgan. "Cave spiders are venomous."

Morgan didn't like it when Theo acted like he knew more about Minecraft than anybody else. "I know cave spiders are venomous," he said, a little less politely than he meant to. "But it can't poison me from way up there."

"Uh," said Theo, "are you sure? Look—"

Morgan looked. **And he saw the spider doing something strange. . . .**

The hostile mob reared back, lifting its front legs and spreading its jaws wide. It made a hissing noise . . . and green mist poured from its mouth. Morgan and Theo were covered in the mist within seconds.

Judging by the mist's sickly green color, Morgan thought it must be a

poisonous fog of some kind. But he didn't feel any effects from it. He looked at Theo, who also seemed uninjured.

Po, however, shrieked in pain and surprise.

Morgan whirled around to see Po splashing around in the lake. "Get them off!" Po cried. "Get them off me!"

It was hard to see much through the fog. But as the water all around Po swirled and splashed, Morgan realized what was wrong. It was the axolotls. They'd become hostile, and they were attacking Po.

"PO, GET OUT OF THERE!" cried Harper.

Jodi didn't wait. She dove into the water in order to drag Po to solid ground. Morgan and Theo ran around the edge of the lake to join the group just as

Jodi and Po hopped out of the water.

"What's happening?" asked Harper. "Where did that green fog come from?"

"There's a spider over there," said Morgan. **"A BIG ONE. DO YOU HAVE A BOW AND ARROWS?"**

"Forget about the spider," said Po. "The axle-what-alls are out to get me!"

The axolotls hopped out of the water. **Their small eyes glowed red in the dark.** Morgan had almost forgotten—unlike fish, amphibians can survive on land for a time.

As the pink one lunged for them, Morgan yelled, "Follow me!"

He led them into the nearest tunnel. He didn't

know where it would take them. He only hoped it would put some distance between them and the spider . . . and the strangely hostile axolotls.

The tunnel twisted and turned. Morgan placed torches down as he ran, but he had to use them sparingly. The darkness was always looming just ahead. **He only hoped he wouldn't lead his friends right over a cliff.** Or what if the tunnel circled back to the cavern, and they ran right into the clutches of that eerie spider?

When Morgan ran out of torches, he stopped, and the others stopped right behind him. The tunnel was narrow, but he could see past his friends. **The axolotls were no longer following them.**

"I THINK WE'RE SAFE," said Morgan. "But let's not take any chances." He placed cobblestone blocks on either side of them, turning the tunnel into a small stone room.

"That was so weird," whispered Po. **"I WAS SO FREAKED OUT BY THE BIG MOB.** When the cute little ones attacked, it caught me by surprise!"

Jodi spoke up. "When I jumped into the water to help you . . . I saw them." She shivered. "Their eyes were red."

"Just like the llama!" said Theo.

"I'll repeat my question from before," said Harper. "*What* is happening here?"

Morgan didn't have an answer. "We should talk about it in the real world, where it's safe. Let's set up our beds." He looked at the torch on the wall. It had been the very last torch in his inventory. He knew they would need more—a *lot* more—if they were to have any hope of surviving down here in the dark.

Chapter 5

WE ALL SCREAM FOR
ICE CREAM, BUT MAYBE
WE SHOULD USE OUR
INSIDE VOICES.

The giant spider was a creepy foe, to be sure. And Po had not *loved* being a target for the axolotls.

But in the bright lights and open spaces of the real world, it was easy to let that stuff go. Besides, Po had a real-world hostile mob to worry about, and her name was Shelly Silver.

And it was time to fight ice cream with ice cream.

"I can't believe you brought a whole ice cream truck to school!" said Theo after the lunch bell rang the next day. He was clearly impressed.

One down, thought Po. *About four hundred more students to go.*

"**It's my cousin's truck,**" explained Po. "She's in high school, and she sells ice cream on the weekends. And she owed me a favor."

"That's a pretty big favor," said Theo. "What did you do, save her cat or something?"

"I fainted," said Po. "Or I pretended to." He smiled at the memory. "We were at a family wedding, and she was desperate to leave early. So I pretended to have a little fainting spell. **She rushed to my 'rescue' and drove me home,** which got her out of there—and made her look like a hero at the same time."

He put his hand to his head and groaned as he slumped in his wheelchair. After a pausing a moment for dramatic effect, he added, "**See. I told you guys I'm a good actor.**"

"But what kind of *politician* are you?" asked Harper, giving him a quick eye roll before getting down to business. "Giving out ice cream to the whole student body is a good way to get everyone's attention. But what are your policies, your ideas?"

Theo added, "You should use this opportunity to actually inform everybody about your platform."

"**Platform?**" echoed Po.

"You know," said Harper. "What kind of changes will you make if you're elected? What promises are you making? **Why are you a better candidate than Shelly Silver?**"

"Um . . . ," said Po. "Well, *my* ice cream is soft serve, which is way better than those little cups."

Harper frowned. "You need to give some thought to this, Po."

"**She has a point,**" said Theo, nodding in agreement with Harper. "If you don't have a plan for being president . . . if you don't have a reason *why* people should vote for you . . . **then all of this is just a popularity contest.**"

"I love popularity contests!" said Po. He saw Theo and Harper exchange a worried look. "Don't worry," he said. "I'll think about what you just said. Consider *that* my first campaign promise."

He pressed the button for the automatic door that led out of the school.

"But right now, I need to make sure my cousin does her part."

Po's cousin, Hope, was in position and ready to go. **She had parked her ice cream truck right across the street, outside Stonesword Library.**

Po wheeled up to the truck and greeted his cousin with a high five.

"Hey, Hope," he said. "Thanks for doing this."

"Anything for you, little cousin," said Hope. "Especially since you'll owe me big-time."

"I figured we'd be *even*," said Po.

Hope chuckled. "That's cute," she said. "But this is a lot of ice cream, we've got *two* family weddings coming up, and I've had enough Chen family country line dances for this lifetime."

Po couldn't argue with that. His grandparents really liked to get down. **It could be weird.**

"Hey, Po!" said a voice. It was Morgan, wearing a bright orange vest over his T-shirt. Despite the sunny outfit, he looked deeply tired.

"Everything's all approved," said Morgan. "It took me most of the night, but I finished the paperwork to get you on the ballot *and* the paperwork that allows you to give out ice cream." **He stifled a yawn.** "The only catch is that we need a crossing guard to make sure students can safely cross the street between the school and the library."

"And you volunteered?" asked Po, understanding now why Morgan was wearing the vest. **"Thanks, Morgan. You're the best!** When I'm president, I'm totally making you my second-in-command."

"You know that's not how it works, right?"

Morgan said, pinching the bridge of his nose. "There's a whole separate election for vice president. And for class secretary, and treasurer . . ."

"**So many rules,**" said Po. "You can tell me all about it later. Right now, I've got an announcement to make."

Po pulled a brand-new megaphone from his backpack, and he held it to his lips. "Free ice cream for all Woodsword students!" he bellowed. "**Come and get it. And vote for me, Po!**"

Morgan winced at the noise, then hurried to stand at the crosswalk.

The school lawn was full of students who had taken their lunches outside. They all perked up at Po's announcement. Most of them stood and stepped forward, drawn by the promise of free dessert.

"Here they come, Hope," said Po. And then, into the megaphone again: "**Vote for Po! Vote for Po!**"

Within seconds, there was a line of students winding halfway down the sidewalk.

Jodi stepped from the crowd. "Hey, Po!" she

said. "I made an announcement in the cafeteria, like you asked. There are a lot more students coming your way." SHE LOOKED OVER AT MORGAN, WHO HAD CAUSED A MINOR TRAFFIC JAM. Cars had begun honking, but with students in the road, there was nothing he could do but hold up his stop sign.

"Maybe I should go help Morgan," she said, and Po just nodded. Into the megaphone, he said, "Vote for PO! VOTE for Po. VOTE for me . . . PO!"

The students in line all cheered.

And there were *a lot* of students in line. Po smiled at the turnout.

And then he frowned. Why wasn't the line moving faster? It was growing longer, and paper

airplanes were taking flight.

Po wheeled to the truck and stuck his head inside. "How's it going, cousin?" he asked.

He was able to guess the answer just by looking at Hope. **His cousin always appeared calm, cool, and collected.** But now, there was a hint of panic in her eyes, and a single drop of sweat running slowly down her cheek.

"All good, cousin!" she said. "It's just . . . you didn't tell me there would be *quite* so many kids."

"Don't think of them as kids," said Po. "Think of them as *votes*. And make sure they're happy. **Extra sprinkles!**"

Hope jabbed a thumbs-up in his direction. But

she did *not* look happy.

"Hey, uh, Po," said Theo. **"Kids are getting a little restless."** A paper airplane hit him in the side of the head. He didn't even bother to try to figure out who threw it. Half the kids in line were throwing things.

"Maybe you should talk to them?" Theo said. "Give a little speech. Something to keep everyone occupied."

Harper checked the time on her phone. "Only, make it quick. Lunch period is over in a few minutes."

Po brought the megaphone up to his mouth. He licked his lips. "Uh, hey, everyone," he said. "I just want to say . . ."

What *did* he want to say? Po's mind went blank. What did politicians talk about?

"Uh, vote for Po!" he said at last.

That didn't seem to do the trick. **This time, he got more jeers than cheers.** The students were rowdier than ever, and the line was still moving far too slowly. Cars and trucks continued to honk from the street.

"What is all this racket?" said a voice. "What's going on out here?"

Po spun his wheelchair around to see Mr. Malory, Stonesword's media specialist. **He looked . . . grumpy.**

"Mr. Malory!" said Po. "I'd offer you an ice cream, sir, but I don't think you get to vote in the student election. . . ."

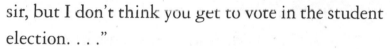

"This noise level is unacceptable," said Mr. Malory. "The media center is for quiet study, and all these voices are coming right through the windows." He looked around the library's courtyard. **"And look at this mess!"**

Po hadn't even noticed, but the trash receptacles were overflowing with garbage. There was recycling in the trash, and trash in the recycling, and extra cups and spoons had been left right on the ground, along with paper airplanes and rubber bands.

"I trust you'll pick this mess up?" said

Mr. Malory. "And see that it's sorted properly?"

"I . . . I'm sure we can make time for that," said Po.

"I have a perfect suggestion," said Mr. Malory. "You and your friends can clean up instead of playing Minecraft in the library today."

Po's heart sank. He could feel the disappointment coming off Theo and the others in waves. And those waves felt like they were crashing right into him.

"Yes, sir," Po said. And just because he thought it couldn't hurt, he added, "Sorry, sir."

Then the bell rang, and the students who hadn't gotten ice cream yet all grumbled and moaned with disappointment.

"I was promised ice cream!" cried a voice from the back of the line. It was Doc Culpepper, their science teacher.

Suddenly, Po felt like he had *a lot* of apologizing to do.

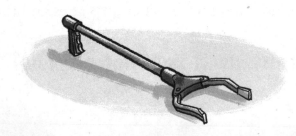

Chapter 6

GETTING OVER THE UNDERGROUND IS HARD TO DO. SURVIVING THE UNDERGROUND MIGHT BE EVEN HARDER!

With everyone working together, Harper knew the after-school cleanup wouldn't take too long. Jodi complained that the job was "icky," Po was upset that his ice cream event had been so chaotic, and **Morgan and Theo were clearly impatient to get back to Minecraft.** But Harper took recycling very seriously, and she made sure that everybody stayed focused on their shared task.

It was a reminder that they made a great team, both in and out of Minecraft.

"Nicely done, kids," said Mr. Malory. He nudged a recycling bin with his foot, checking that everything had been sorted correctly. "You still have time to use the computers before your parents arrive, if you want. **I set aside the VR goggles, just in case.**"

"Thanks, Mr. Malory," said Harper, and Morgan and the others whooped with excitement and hurried into the library.

Mr. Malory shushed them, but he was laughing as he did it.

As soon as the kids spawned in Minecraft, Po twirled around to show off his new avatar skin. **"I'M READY FOR ADVENTURE . . . AND DRESSED FOR SUCCESS!"** he said. He looked like a politician, with a suit and tie and slicked-back hair.

"Nice!" said Jodi. "Maybe we should build a

replica White House for you. Ooh! Except we'll make it out of wool!"

"That sounds . . . interesting. And highly flammable," said Theo. **"BUT LET'S NOT FORGET THERE COULD BE A GIANT CAVE SPIDER PROWLING AROUND DOWN HERE."**

Harper nodded. "Morgan and Po said they saw that green mist before the spider appeared last time," she said. "That information could help us avoid the spider while we find a way back to the surface."

"We *could* do that," said Morgan. "But I think we want to do the opposite. **I THINK WE WANT TO FIND THE SPIDER."**

Jodi put her cube hand to his head, as if checking his temperature. "Are you feeling all right, big brother? Because you are *not* making sense."

"Hear me out," said Morgan. "We were all excited to explore these caves, so we got distracted. But we're *supposed* to be looking for strange mobs. The mobs that used to be the Evoker King."

"YOU THINK THAT TERROR-ANTULA IS ONE OF THOSE MOBS?" asked Po.

"We are *not* calling it that," said Theo.

Morgan nodded. "Whatever we call it, it has to be what we're looking for," he said. "We've all seen dozens of cave spiders, but we've never encountered one like that. And it didn't just *look* unique . . . **IT HAD SOME KIND OF SPECIAL POWER.** I'm pretty sure it was the reason those axolotls attacked Po."

"I've already forgiven the sweet little things," said Po, pretending to wipe away a tear.

"So my big brother isn't as fevered as we thought," Jodi said. "But what do we do next?"

"We need a plan," Theo agreed.

"I think we need more information first," said Harper. "Let's try to find this spider. If we're quiet enough, maybe we can observe it from a safe distance. Then we can learn whether it really is doing things a normal spider can't do."

"That works for me," said Morgan. "We'll know if we're getting close when we see the green mist, so it shouldn't be able to catch us by surprise."

"And we can explore the caves in the meantime!" said Po. "SCORE!"

Harper had to hand it to Po: he was right to be excited about the caves. **There was more to see underground than she had ever expected.**

"Wow," said Po as they stepped out of a tunnel and entered another large cavern. **"LOOK OUT FOR SPIKES!"**

"Those aren't spikes," said Harper. She looked at the icicle-like cones of stone that filled the cavern. "That's dripstone. The spiky shapes it makes are called stalactites and stalagmites," she said.

"I always forget which is which," said Morgan.

"I have a trick for remembering," said Harper.

"Stalactites hang down from the ceiling—like a capital letter T. Stalagmites, on the other hand, jut out from the ground—like a capital M."

Theo grinned. **"THAT'S A REALLY CLEVER TRICK, HARPER,"** he said.

Harper was glad her avatar couldn't blush. "Thanks," she said.

"DOES ANYBODY ELSE HEAR THAT SOUND?" asked Po. "It's almost like music. . . ."

Harper listened intently. Po was right. There was a faint tinkling noise nearby. "I think it's coming from the other side of this wall," she said, pressing her ear to a wall of dark gray stone.

Theo examined the wall. "That looks like basalt," he said. "But I've only ever seen basalt in the Nether before now."

"NOT QUITE!" said Morgan, and his eyes went wide. "If that's smooth basalt, then I know exactly what's making that sound." He pulled a pickaxe from his inventory. "Stand back!"

Morgan struck the smooth basalt wall with his pickaxe. "Smooth basalt is normally found in the Nether, **BUT WHEN YOU DO FIND IT IN THE OVERWORLD, YOU FIND THIS. . . .**" He dug a few blocks deep, then stepped aside to let everyone see what he'd uncovered. It looked like a hidden room made of glittering purple gemstones.

"Is that amethyst?" asked Harper.

Morgan nodded. **"IT'S A WHOLE GEODE OF AMETHYST."**

Jodi gasped. "It's so pretty!" She ran through the opening Morgan had made. Harper watched as Jodi spun around in joy, surrounded by gems. "Just think of the artwork we could make with this," she said.

Morgan hefted his pickaxe. **"THEN LET'S GET MINING,"** he said.

Chapter 7

THANK YOU FOR YOUR HOSPITALITY, VILLAGERS! I ESPECIALLY ENJOYED IT WHEN YOU STOPPED HITTING ME.

Theo led the way back to the surface.

While Morgan and Jodi had mined the amethyst, Theo and Harper had done some exploring. They'd found iron, copper, lapis lazuli **. . . and even a few emeralds.**

It had been Theo's idea to head back to the village they had seen before. There, they would be able to trade their emeralds for something useful.

It took longer than he expected to reach the top. **They were deep belowground,** and they couldn't dig straight up, since they couldn't fly. (Theo wondered if he could come up with a mod to change that.) He had to cut a zigzagging diagonal path up through countless earthen blocks, while Harper placed torches behind him.

He was cutting blind, and that was always risky, because you could accidentally open a hole right into a raging river of water—or worse, lava. Theo kept some cobblestone handy just in case he needed to quickly plug a hole. But he was lucky. He cut through stone, and then through dirt, and finally, the night sky appeared just overhead.

As they emerged onto the surface, it took a moment for everyone to get their bearings. There was the mountain—and there, at its base, was the village. **They walked quickly across the plain, eager to avoid any unnecessary fights with the hostile mobs that prowled the Overworld at night.**

As they reached the outskirts of the village,

Harper bounced on her blocky feet. "What should we buy?" she asked. "I had a few emeralds already, so we should have enough for something good. **MAYBE AN ENCHANTED BOOK? OR REDSTONE DUST!** We don't have much of it."

Morgan nodded. "Let's see what the villagers have," he said. "I didn't see a librarian when we were here before. But their cleric might have redstone dust for sale."

As the others spread out among the villagers, **Theo saw Po placing a sign in the dirt.** In glowing letters, it read VOTE FOR PO!

"Where in the world did you get that?" Theo asked.

"I crafted it myself," said Po. "While you guys were mining for ores and amethyst, **I FOUND SOME GLOW SQUID. THEY DROPPED GLOWING INK!**"

"I don't think these villagers get a vote," Theo said, but Po didn't seem to be listening.

Harper had already found the cleric, a serious-looking mob with green eyes and a purple robe. While they haggled, Theo looked around for a librarian.

It was difficult to see anything, though. **The fog was partially blocking the light of the torches.**

"Wait a minute," said Theo. **"WHERE DID THIS FOG COME FROM?"**

Suddenly, the cleric's green eyes turned red. The villager lunged at Harper, bashing into her with a blocky shoulder.

"Hey!" said Harper. "What gives?"

"Oh no," said Jodi. She backed away from a red-eyed farmer. "Not this again!"

Theo pulled a sword from his inventory. "Should we fight them?" he asked. "It feels wrong."

Harper stood her ground as the cleric made another lunge at her. "They're . . . super weak, actually," she said. "I don't think this cleric is even doing any damage to my health."

The farmer was joined by a fisherman, and several other angry villagers were leaving their homes to join the crowd.

"I'm almost afraid they're going to hurt *themselves*," said Po. "They're all worked up!"

"I agree," said Morgan. "There's no point fighting them. Let's retreat and see what happens."

THEO FOLLOWED THE OTHERS AS THEY FLED PAST THE OUTSKIRTS OF THE VILLAGE. Some of the villagers gave chase, but they soon gave up. Their eyes still glowed red in the night, but they didn't seem interested in pursuing the kids.

"I wonder what they'll do now," said Theo. He couldn't help but imagine the programming that determined how villagers would act. **And he tried to imagine how that program had been warped and rewritten by the spider's mind-poisoning fog.**

As they watched from a distance, they saw the villagers form a single-file line and leave their village. It looked as if they were hypnotized and following the commands of some unheard voice.

"Where are they going?" whispered Po.

"MAYBE THEY HEARD SOMEONE WAS GIVING OUT FREE ICE CREAM?" teased Jodi.

"I think I know where they're going," said Harper. "Look! They're headed right for the hole. The one we climbed out of a few minutes ago."

As usual, Harper was right. Theo watched as the villagers descended into the darkness, one after another.

"THAT IS AN EERIE SIGHT," said Morgan. "I hope they'll be okay. . . ."

"It's the spider," said Po. "It has to be. **IT'S CAUGHT THEM IN ITS PSYCHIC WEB!**"

"But what does it want with all those villagers?" asked Jodi. "Should we follow them?"

Harper shook her head. "We got a late start today, remember? We don't have time to follow them now. We'll have to try to track them down tomorrow."

"I GUESS WE HAVE A WHOLE EMPTY VILLAGE TO OURSELVES," said Morgan. **"PLENTY OF SPACE TO SET UP OUR BEDS."**

Theo felt uneasy, but he knew this problem would simply have to wait.

"Let's make sure we come back as soon as we can tomorrow," he said.

Po nodded. "I'm with Theo. Because I think I know why the spider wants those villagers." He gave his friends a long, serious look. "It seems to me . . . **LIKE THE SPIDER IS BUILDING AN ARMY!**"

Chapter 8

IF YOU LOVE YOUR JOB, YOU'LL NEVER WORK A DAY IN YOUR LIFE. IF YOU HATE YOUR JOB . . . TOUGH!

"ALL RIGHT, Block Headz. Face front! Your assignments . . . are ready!"

Po put *energy* into his words. The ice cream truck had not been the grand slam he'd hoped for. But there was plenty of time to get his campaign in shape. **He could still win all the votes he needed to become class president!**

And his friends had said they wanted to help any way they could, right? So he'd take them up on that.

The good news: They all looked excited and ready to begin. **The bad news:** They had a lot of their *own* ideas already.

"I've already been sketching some posters," said Jodi. "And I'm going to do the graphics for the website that Theo is building."

"I'm putting together polls so we can have accurate models to make predictions," said Harper. **"And I've got Ash on the phone, like you asked.** She said she'll help however she can."

Harper propped her smartphone up against a juice box. Their friend and fellow Minecraft fanatic, Ash Kapoor, waved at them from the screen.

"It's good to see you, Ash," said Po. "But everybody . . . slow your roll! I'm glad you're all eager to help, but I already came up with everyone's assignments."

Morgan gave him a suspicious look. "Really?"

"Posters and websites and that stuff—it's all kind of basic," said Po. "We need to think bigger. Bolder. We need a campaign that's truly one-of-a-kind!"

"Okay," Harper said, crossing her arms. "What do you have in mind?"

"Well, let's start with you, Harper," he said. "You know how our morning announcements are all automated with Doc's technology? **I want you to hack into the system and replace the normal announcements with pro-Po slogans.**"

Harper frowned. "I'm pretty sure that's against the rules . . . like, *all* the rules," she said. "And anyway, that sounds like a programming job, and

that's Theo's area of expertise, not mine."

"Unfortunately, Theo will be busy," said Po. "I need him to link up with my basketball teammates and lead them in a flash mob. I'm imagining coordinated dancing through the halls of the school! Music, fireworks, go wild!"

"Me? Dance?" said Theo, going pale. "In *public*?"

"And fireworks indoors?" said Morgan.

"I haven't forgotten about you, Morgan," said Po. "You did such a good job on all that paperwork, and I want you to know how much I appreciate it. Now I need you to put those skills to use and bake some cookies! If everyone in school gets a cookie, they'll forget all about that ice cream disaster."

"Wait a minute," said Morgan. "What does paperwork have to do with baking?"

"And what does baking have to do with Morgan?" asked Jodi. **"The last time he tried to bake something, he set our kitchen on fire.** And somehow the cake was *still* undercooked."

Po turned to Jodi. "You're good at noticing details like that, Jodi. You're a master spy, after all." He grinned. "So I want you to spy on Shelly

Silver. I need to know every move she makes. If she puts up ten posters, I'll put twenty ads in the paper. If she hands out candy, I'll give away whole chocolate bars. Name-brand chocolate bars. Whatever it takes!"

Jodi frowned and said under her breath, "I *spy* someone who is being *ridiculous*."

"I'm almost afraid to ask what you have in mind for me, Po," Ash said.

Po shrugged. "Easy. You're here for emotional support," he said. **"You're good at it!"**

Ash breathed an immediate sigh of relief and said, "I can handle that."

Just then, a gleam of reflected light caught Po's eye. Morgan was eating gelatin with a shiny spoon. **Po recognized that spoon.**

"**Morgan!**" he said. "How could you?"

Morgan froze, a spoonful of gelatin halfway to his mouth. "How could I what?"

"How could you use one of *her* spoons?"

Morgan looked down at the spoon, then back at Po. The gelatin quivered.

"It's just a spoon," he said. "It doesn't mean anything."

Po harrumphed. *Just a spoon!*

"Wow, Po," said Harper. "**I feel like you have a lot in common with that spider mob we're after.** If only you could fill the hallways with a mind-altering gas. Then you could just hypnotize everyone into voting for you."

Po had to admit . . . he didn't hate that idea. "How does the science on that work, exactly? Would Doc have something we could use?"

"Po!" exclaimed Harper. "**I was only joking!**"

Ash cleared her throat. "As the emotional support expert," she said, "I'm feeling like your campaign is getting . . . a little out of hand, Po. Can we talk about this?"

"It'll have to wait," said Po. "I've got to head

to homeroom and get Baron Sweetcheeks ready for his photo op." **He held up the cutest little "Vote for Po!" T-shirt in the world.**

"He's the campaign mascot, and I want his image on everything—stickers, mugs, water bottles, you name it. Because who wouldn't want to vote with the Baron?"

"There's no way Baron Sweetcheeks agreed to that," Jodi said under her breath.

"When will it end?" Morgan muttered.

"When I'm president," said Po, **and he waved the tiny T-shirt like a flag.** "And not a minute before!"

Chapter 9

STRAIGHT INTO THE SPIDER'S WEB! WHAT COULD GO WRONG? PROBABLY NOTHING—EXCEPT A GIANT SPIDER!

Despite the unresolved disagreements from their lunchtime meeting, Theo and the others all agreed to return to Minecraft as soon as possible. **The moment the end-of-day bell rang, they hurried to the library and put on their VR headsets.**

They spawned in the village. Theo had hoped to find the villagers back where they belonged. But the houses remained empty. The streets were silent.

That meant the villagers were still underground. And the kids had no choice but to follow them.

"Let's cut down some trees first," said Harper.

"We're going through a lot of torches down there."

As they climbed back down the hole that Theo had cut through the earth, **he readied his sword and thought back to the last major foe they'd faced.** They'd called it the Endermonster, and they had not been able to defeat it by fighting it. Instead, they'd trapped the mob in a pit, and then Theo had talked to it— *connected* with it. He'd made it understand that they meant no harm.

Would their conflict with this strange spider work similarly?

"I THINK WE SHOULD TRY TO TRAP THE SPIDER," he said. "Like we did with the Endermonster. That way, we can maybe find out what it wants . . . *without* hurting it." Theo remembered the other lesson he'd learned on that adventure: how to be a team player. "That's just my idea," he added. "What do you all think?"

"It makes sense to me," said Harper.

"Do you want to get it to chase us?" asked Jodi.

Theo nodded. **"AND WE'LL LEAD THE MOB RIGHT INTO A WAITING PIT."**

"I bet it'll be even easier with the spider," said Po. "At least it can't teleport!"

"But we'll be running through the fog, if it's chasing us," Morgan reminded them. "I think it's a good plan, Theo. We'll just need to be careful."

They descended to the dripstone cavern where they'd mined for materials the day before. "The villagers must have come through here," said Theo. "I didn't see any other paths the entire way down."

"We came from that direction the other day,"

said Harper, pointing. **"AND WE KNOW THAT'S A DEAD END, SINCE WE BLOCKED THE TUNNEL WITH COBBLESTONE."**

"So it's that way," said Morgan, pointing at the only other exit from the cavern. "They had to have gone through there."

Theo gulped. It was easy to be brave when they were just talking about a plan. But now, as the dark pressed closer to them and their encounter with the spider drew near . . . he felt a trickle of fear run through his avatar.

HARPER STEPPED INTO THE MIDDLE OF THE CAVERN, AND SHE PULLED A PICKAXE FROM HER INVENTORY. "Spiders can jump, so we need a pretty deep hole this time," she said.

"I'd better free some space in my inventory for all the dirt we're going to kick up," said Po. He jabbed a couple of glowing "Vote for Po" signs into the ground.

"How many of those things did he make?" asked Theo to no one in particular.

Harper sighed, then forced a smile. **"LET'S START DIGGING,"** she said.

The pit had been dug, and Theo crept along a tunnel toward the spider. The tunnel was two blocks wide, so there was just enough room for two of them to walk side by side. Theo was in the lead with Harper.

They'd agreed not to use too many torches. **They didn't want the spider to see them coming. But it was dark.** Theo walked with one hand in front of him so he wouldn't bump into anything.

He didn't even realize that the tunnel had begun to fill with mist until Harper pointed it out. "We must be getting close," she whispered. And then, suddenly, she gripped him and pulled him back.

The spider was directly ahead of them, standing in the middle of a large cavern. The only light came from the slight bluish glow of two small ponds. **Theo guessed there were glow squids in those pools.** He squinted and saw axolotls swimming alongside them.

Those aquatic creatures were not the only mobs

present. The spider was surrounded by red-eyed villagers, sheep, rabbits, and more. Theo saw a llama, and he was pretty sure it was the same llama that had attacked Jodi. **As for the villagers, they seemed to be treating the spider like a king.** They offered it fresh-baked bread and emeralds. Theo half expected to see them massage the mob's eight big block feet next!

"Po was right. **IT IS BUILDING AN ARMY,**" Theo whispered.

"I don't know," whispered Harper. "They all seem sort of . . . peaceful. They look more like worshippers or servants than soldiers."

"This doesn't change anything," whispered Morgan. "Our plan's still a good one. **PO, DO YOU**

WANT TO DO THE HONORS?"

Po smiled. "You know I do."

"Then make some noise," said Morgan.

Po stepped in front of Theo and cleared his throat. Then he yelled at the top of his lungs: **"VOTE FOR PO!!"**

The spider snapped to attention. The large mob hissed, lifting one of its long legs and pointing right at them.

"Here it comes," said Theo. **"RUN!"**

They dove back into the tunnel, this time with Jodi at the front and Po bringing up the rear. Theo was right in the middle. He glanced back, and he could see Morgan and Po right behind him, but through the swirling mist it was impossible to see if the spider was near or far.

They ran through the thickening fog.
They turned left. Then they turned right.

Then Theo thought: Wait. That's wrong.

"Are we lost?" he said.

"I think I took a wrong turn!" cried Jodi from ahead of him.

"Well, we can't go back now," said Harper.

"JUST KEEP GOING!"

As soon as they stopped talking, Theo heard the unmistakable sounds of pursuit. There was definitely something following them. It sounds like a whole *lot* of somethings, in fact.

"HERE THEY COME," warned Morgan.

"Run away!" Po cried frantically. "Run away, run away, run away!"

"Forget this!" said Theo. Sometimes being a team player just wasn't worth the trouble. He took a quick glance at the compass he carried, which gave him his bearings. Then he took out a diamond pickaxe, which would allow him to cut through stone in no time at all. **"I'M MAKING A NEW TUNNEL,"** he said. "Everybody follow me!"

Theo's sense of direction proved true. He only had to hack through five layers of stone before he cut right through to the chamber where they'd begun. Their pit was nearby.

"Hurry!" he said.

Out of the tunnel, they were able to spread out at last, and they ran side by side toward the pit. **They leaped and their pursuers fell**

into the deep hole in the ground, just as they'd planned.

Only it wasn't the horrible spider who had pursued them. **It was dozens of bunny rabbits.**

"It didn't even follow us, did it?" said Theo. "It sent these rabbits to do its dirty work!"

"And you, bunnies?" said Jodi, heartbroken. "The spider turned *you* against us, too?"

Harper leaned over the pit. "Look at their eyes, though," she said. "They're back to normal." She stood again. "That's good news. It means the

spider's control wears off at a distance. Probably as soon as there's none of that mist around."

Jodi eyed the bunnies with suspicion. "I don't know. **I JUST DON'T KNOW IF I CAN TRUST THEIR CUTE LITTLE FACES.**"

Po patted her on the head. She'd been through a lot this week.

"You know, the bunnies *are* awfully cute," said Theo. "Maybe the spider isn't such a bad mob if it's gathering fuzzy animals and villagers instead of bats and zombies." He rubbed the top of his head. **"MAYBE PO'S ARMY THEORY DOESN'T HOLD UP AFTER ALL."**

And then a sound erupted from the tunnels. It was a sound of sadness and desperation, and it sent a shiver across Theo's digital skin.

"It's . . . *wailing*," said Harper.

"It sounds sad," said Jodi. **"DO YOU THINK IT MISSES THE BUNNIES?"**

"Sad or not, it sounds awfully creepy to me," said Po.

"Me too," said Theo. "I think we should retreat to the village."

Morgan nodded. "This plan was a bust," he said. "We have to come up with something else."

Chapter 10

IF YOUR RIVAL REACHES ACROSS THE AISLE . . . GIVE HER A COOKIE.

It was a beautiful morning outside in the real world. Jodi, Harper, and Theo were together, **sitting beneath a tree. Jodi was sketching Minecraft rabbits on graph paper.** She wouldn't let some creepy, kooky Minecraft mob ruin her love of bunnies. Or llamas. **Or axolotls!** She'd never known how cute amphibians could be. She'd looked them up online and confirmed that they were just as adorable in

real life as they were in pixels.

Jodi glanced at Harper. She was drawing, too, and Theo was looking over her shoulder. They were putting their heads together on a new plan to deal with the spider.

Morgan was nearby, rushing to finish his homework. He'd spent all night making cookies. They were unappetizing, but at least he hadn't set the kitchen on fire. To Jodi, that was progress.

"Hi, everybody," said a voice, **and Jodi looked up to see Shelly Silver standing over them.** "Can I join you for a minute?"

Jodi was surprised. She'd never talked with Shelly—and despite Po, she'd certainly never spied on

her. So what was Shelly doing here?

"Uh...sure, you can join us," said Morgan. He obviously felt awkward. Jodi even saw him look around to make sure Po wasn't nearby. But there was still twenty minutes before the first bell, and Po usually didn't get to school this early.

Harper set aside her notebook. "Have a seat, Shelly," she said. "What's on your mind?"

Shelly smiled. She had a nice smile, Jodi thought. Friendly.

"Thanks," Shelly said, and she folded her legs to sit on the grass. "I know you're all friends with Po, so I won't try to convince you to vote for me. But I'm trying to speak with *every* student before the election." She took out a pocket-sized spiral

notepad and a glitter pen with a big pink pompom on the end. "That way, if I *am* elected, I'll have an idea what everyone cares about."

"What we care about?" echoed Theo.

"Yeah," said Shelly. "You know. **What's your number-one issue?** What would you like to see change around here?"

Theo thought about it. "I'd like the computer lab back," he said.

"Ditto," said Morgan. "Our computer equipment should be in the school, where we can keep an eye on it."

Jodi knew they were worried that keeping their VR headsets in the library meant that someone else would use them.

"I care about recycling," said Harper. "And other sustainable practices."

"Oh, me too, actually!" said Shelly. "Woodsword is pretty good about all that, but it could be better. I have a lot of ideas."

That got a big smile from Harper.

"What do you think about the upcoming block party?" she asked.

Jodi understood immediately why Shelly was asking. The block party was an annual event—an after-school party for all the students and their families. But some students had decided the party was a big waste of money. They argued that the money could be spent on important improvements around the school.

"I think it's a waste," said Harper, and Theo nodded in agreement.

"No, I love the block party!" said Morgan. "I've been looking forward to it all year."

Jodi noticed Shelly writing their responses in her notebook. She was really paying attention to what they cared about.

And she had a sudden, sinking feeling . . . that Po might not win the election.

"Oh!" said Shelly. Her eyes had landed on Morgan's containers full of cookies. **"Are you selling cookies?"**

"Yeah," said Morgan. He squirmed a little. "Uh, they're for Po's campaign, though. Sorry."

Shelly shrugged. "That's okay."

She'd been so nice, though, that Morgan let

her have her choice of cookie anyway. She chose one and bit into it immediately. Jodi watched as Shelly's expression went from excitement . . . to confusion . . . to mild disgust. She chewed for several seconds, then winced as she swallowed. "That is . . . an *interesting* cookie," she said.

"I'm sorry!" said Morgan, knowing the cookies were terrible. "I think I mixed up the baking powder and the baking soda. *But why is baking soda a powder?* It's so confusing!"

They all laughed, Shelly the loudest of all. She didn't eat the rest of the cookie, but she politely wrapped it in a napkin and placed it in her purse, as if she might get back to it later.

Po saw it all. Hidden behind a large oak tree, he watched in silence as Shelly approached his friends. He saw them invite her to sit down. He saw them laugh and smile with her like they were having the best time in the world.

What was Shelly Silver up to?

And why were his friends going along with it?

Po never would have believed it if he hadn't seen it with his own eyes. But there could be only one explanation: *Shelly Silver was turning Po's own friends against him.*

Chapter 11

A CHIP OFF THE OLD BLOCK HEADZ. LET'S JUST HOPE THESE CHIPS DON'T END UP IN A BATCH OF MORGAN'S COOKIES!

After school, the kids met up in Minecraft. Everything was just as usual.

Except for one big difference. **This time, Po watched his teammates with anger and suspicion.**

They were standing in one of the village's many abandoned houses, where they'd set up their beds in a neat row. "Theo and I have a new plan," said Harper. "Or a new version of the old plan."

"We're still going to trap the spider," said Theo. "But not in a pit this time. We're going to build a trap . . . **USING REDSTONE.**"

Po scoffed. "Redstone is too complicated,"

he said. "Here's my plan: Let's go to the Nether. Let's get some netherite. Let's craft some powerful weapons and armor and defeat the spider in a direct attack!"

"But we don't want to hurt it," said Theo. "Remember, it contains a piece of the Evoker King's code. **WE NEED THAT CODE TO PUT OUR FRIEND BACK TOGETHER.**"

"If we trap it, we can find a way to communicate

with it," said Harper. "Maybe we can convince it to give us what we need, like we did with the Endermonster."

"BESIDES, THE SPIDER HASN'T ACTUALLY HURT US," Jodi added. "It keeps using its mobs to chase us away when we get too close. Maybe it isn't so bad, really."

Po felt hurt that nobody was listening to him. "Did you guys ask *Shelly Silver* what she thought about your plan?" he asked.

MORGAN'S JAW DROPPED IN SURPRISE.

"Yeah, that's right," said Po. "I saw you all talking this morning. She was even taking notes! What did you tell her?"

"It wasn't like that," Morgan said. "She was just asking us some questions about the school. About our opinions . . ."

"Sounds like she's spying on my campaign," said Po. He looked at Jodi. "Speaking of spying, have you learned anything I can use, Jodi?"

Jodi put her blocky fists on her hips. **"I REFUSE TO USE MY DETECTIVE POWERS FOR EVIL!"** she said. "Shelly is a nice person."

"SHE'S MY COMPETITOR," said Po.

"She can be both of those things!" argued Jodi.

"That's enough, everybody," said Harper, and she stepped between them. "Let's remember we're all on the same team."

"Are we, though?" said Po. He frowned at Morgan. "Or were those inedible cookies part of your plan to sabotage me?"

"THEY'RE NOT INEDIBLE!" Morgan argued. "They're even pretty good if you dip them in mustard."

"What's going on here?" said a voice from the doorway.

They all turned to see a familiar avatar. "Ash!" said Jodi. "Thank goodness you're here!"

Ash smiled. "It's always good to see you guys." Then her smile fell away. "But I hate to see you like *this*. You'll never topple that tyrant if you don't work together."

Theo chuckled. **"WHEN YOU SAY 'TYRANT,' ARE YOU TALKING ABOUT THE SPIDER? OR PO?"**

Po felt a rush of anger. "I'm not a tyrant!" he

said. "I just want things to go my way for once!"

Everyone was quiet after that. Po was normally such a happy guy. **His anger had caught everyone by surprise.**

"I think we all need to take a time out," said Ash. "There's no way we should be going up against a hostile boss mob in this state."

"I'll make it easy for you guys," said Po, and he disconnected without another word.

Po exited the library before his friends could disconnect and follow him. He knew Ash was right—he needed a time-out. He needed to *breathe*, before he said something he would regret.

And then, suddenly, he had a microphone shoved right into his face.

"I'm Ned Brant with the *Woodsword Chronicler*," said the student on the holding the microphone. "I'm doing profiles on our candidates. What can you tell me about your platform?"

"Wait, what?" said Po. His mind was still reeling

from the argument. He wasn't at all prepared to talk to a student reporter. "I don't know."

"You don't know anything about your platform?" said the reporter.

"I mean, yeah, of course I do," said Po. **"Look, I'm just trying to have a good time. You can print that! Call me the happy fun-time candidate."**

The reporter frowned. "But what about the issues? Where do you stand?"

Po nodded as if he took the question very

seriously. "I have a lot of opinions about a lot of different issues. Pretty much all the issues, actually."

Nailed it, thought Po.

"What about the block party?" said Ned.

"Sure," said Po. "That sounds fun. Let's do it!"

Ned shook his head. "No, I mean where do you stand on the debate? A growing number of students believe it's a waste of the school's money."

"They do?" said Po. "Then we'll just cancel it."

"Cancel it?" echoed the reporter. "You're saying that if you're elected class president . . . the block party will be canceled?"

Po hesitated for a moment. **He felt that maybe he'd said the wrong thing.** But this reporter had just said that students weren't happy about the block party. So his was obviously the right answer. Right?

"Yes," said Po. "Consider it a campaign promise. Now get out there and spread the word, Ned." As Po wheeled away, he shouted over his shoulder, **"Vote for Po!"**

Chapter 12

EXTRA! EXTRA! READ ALL ABOUT IT . . . SO YOU'LL KNOW WHAT EVERYBODY'S YELLING ABOUT!

Po couldn't wait to arrive at school the next morning. He was pretty sure he had nailed that interview with the student reporter. **His whole campaign was about to turn around.**

In a way, he was right. But not at all in the way he expected.

He noticed the looks and the whispers as soon as he approached the school. Po was generally a popular guy. People tended to say hello to him in the hallways. Today, it was the opposite. Nobody seemed to want to talk to him.

They all seemed to be talking *about* him instead.

Finally, Po's teammate Ricky approached him.

"Dude," said Ricky, "is it true?"

"Is what true?" asked Po. "What's going on around here?"

"The newspaper ran a story," said Ricky. He held up his phone to show Po the digital edition of that morning's *Woodsword Chronicler.* "They're saying you want to cancel the block party!"

"That's not true," said Po. He thought about it for a second. "Well, it's *kind of* true. But I just said that because that's what people want me to do!"

"Which people?" said Ricky. "I was looking forward to that party." **He waved around the hallway at all the glaring, eavesdropping students.** "And I'm not the only one."

"Fine," said Po. "Okay. No problem. I can fix this." He pulled his megaphone from his backpack and held it to his mouth. "Attention, everybody! There's no need to panic! I'm reversing my position on the block party. **Po is the pro-party candidate!**" He lowered the megaphone, then quickly raised it once more. "Vote for Po!" he added.

"Are you serious?" said a student. "We need that money for repairs around here. The door to my locker just fell off!"

"That's because you're always slamming it shut, *Megan*," said another girl.

"We should spend the money on repairs!" someone shouted.

"No!" said Ricky. "We study hard all year long. **We deserve a party!**"

"I'm with Ricky," said Doc Culpepper, stepping

out of her lab. "Things are too tense around here. A fête is just the thing."

Ms. Minerva, Po's homeroom teacher, crossed her arms. For some reason, she was soaking wet. "Don't be foolish, Doc," she said. "You know better than anyone that we need new equipment around here."

"Bah," said Doc. **"I can just fix the old equipment."**

"Like you fixed the sprinkler system on the lawn?" said Minerva. She wrung water out of her blouse. "Because I think it's still got a few bugs."

Doc turned to Po. "Well, Po?" she asked. "What do *you* say?"

All eyes were back on Po. Everyone disagreed . . . but they *all* wanted him to be on their side.

Po had absolutely no idea what to do. He hated to admit it—**but if he had the spider's mind-zap mist power right now, he just might use it.**

Suddenly, a clear voice cut through the silence. "Give Po some space!"

To Po's surprise, his defender was none other than Shelly Silver.

"It isn't fair to catch him off guard like this," she said. **"A politician needs time to consider their position on complicated issues."** She waved her notebook in the air. "I've been thinking about it all week, and I'm *still* considering where I stand."

Po felt miserable. He liked making people *happy*. And here he was, making them angry and frustrated instead. And who came to his defense? Not Ricky. Not the Minecraft crew. No, it was his political rival speaking up for him.

That made him want to lash out.

"You sound awfully indecisive, Shelly," he said, loud enough that everyone would hear him. "Don't you think we need a class president who's daring and *decisive*?"

Shelly didn't seem to know what to say to that. Her mouth dropped open.

Po saw his chance. **This was his opportunity,** at last, to prove to everyone that he was the right man for the job.

"Shelly Silver," he said. **"I challenge you to a debate!"**

Chapter 13

BE CAREFUL WHAT YOU TRAP FOR. YOU JUST MIGHT CATCH IT!

"A DEBATE?!" said Morgan. "Po, are you sure that's the best idea?"

"No, I'm not," Po admitted. **"But I panicked. I wasn't thinking!"** It was after school, and Morgan and Po were in the library, waiting for the others to join them. "I've been doing that a lot lately, haven't I?" he said after a moment. "Speaking without thinking first, I mean. I'm sorry I lost my temper yesterday."

Morgan sighed. "Yeah, well. **I'm sorry I pretended my cookies weren't terrible.** They really are inedible."

Po laughed. "I appreciate that you made the

effort. And I appreciate their obsidian-like quality."

Morgan smiled. It felt like everything was back to normal. Po was being his old, fun self again. "But seriously, Po," he said. "What's been going on with you? Are you, you know . . . all

right?"

Po took another moment to think before answering. "I want to win the election," he said. "I want it really badly. I don't even know why— **I just hate the thought of losing."**

"Everybody likes to win," said Morgan. "But sometimes that makes us fight the wrong battles."

Po blinked. "Morgan, that sounded seriously wise!"

Morgan blushed and confessed, "I'm actually just quoting something Ash said yesterday."

"Well, if you're going to steal," said Po, "steal from the best."

Theo, Harper, and Jodi arrived. **The five of them all put their headsets on at the same time—as a team.**

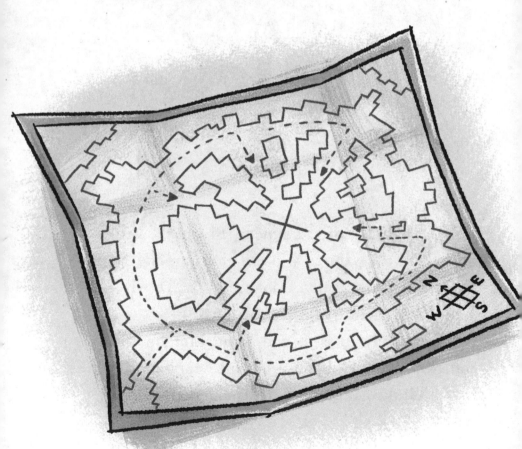

In the caverns beneath the Overworld, the trap had been set. Now they needed to lure the spider out of its hiding place. Po followed his friends through the dark tunnel that led to the spider's den.

"I can't believe we're going *toward* the creepy-crawly," said Jodi.

"It's okay," said Ash. **"WE'VE GOT EACH OTHER BACKS."**

"Yeah," said Morgan. "Except for the part of the plan where we're all alone . . ."

Po was nervous about that, too. But he trusted Harper and Theo, who had come up with this whole idea. They had figured out where to dig the tunnels and where to place the redstone dust. The blueprint that showed where everything should go looked a little bit like a spider's web. **That had made Po giggle . . . nervously.**

They were going to catch the spider in a web of their own. But it was a very big spider.

They all walked slowly as they approached the

den. The strange green mist swirled all around them.

And there, surrounded by its loyal mobs, was the spider.

Po whispered, "Okay, there he is. Lucky us! Now what?"

Harper grinned. "Now we make a mess. **EVERYBODY, THROW YOUR POTIONS!**"

Po didn't need to be told twice. He threw the Splash Potion that Harper had given him, and the other kids did the same. The potions glowed purple as they spun through the air. **When the bottles shattered, the liquid splashed the spider, the villagers, the axolotls, and all the other mobs with Slowness.**

Now the mobs would be easy to outrun for the next ninety seconds.

They needed to make those ninety seconds matter.

"Come and get us!" Theo said, and the spider turned its red eyes on them and hissed. It was the sound of paper being torn to shreds in anger. In seconds, the entire group of mobs stepped forward. Their eyes, too, flashed red as they gave chase.

"HERE THEY COME," said Ash.

"Be careful what you wish for, I guess," said Jodi.

"Let's go," said Harper. "Follow me!"

As a group, they turned and ran down the tunnel. But then Morgan turned right down a side path.

And a little farther up, Jodi turned left.

Po felt a little rush of nervousness as he took a

different side path of his own. He knew their plan relied on this. They needed to separate that big crowd of mobs, and the best way to do that was to split up. Still, he was anxious about being alone in the dark.

He looked back and saw that several of the villagers had turned to follow him. **They were moving slowly because of the potion, so it was easy for Po to stay out of their reach.** In fact, he slowed down a little bit. He didn't want to lose them.

He let them get closer. **Closer . . .**

And then he hit a lever, and an iron door swung closed behind him.

The villagers threw themselves against the iron door—*thump-thump-thump*—but there was nothing they could do. They were trapped . . . and now the spider's army was a little bit smaller than before.

"SEE YOU LATER!" Po said, cackling. He was starting to feel good about the plan.

Po followed his tunnel back to the central cavern. Harper, Theo, and Jodi were already there.

"How'd it go?" Harper asked.

"I trapped some villagers," Po answered.

Harper nodded. "Great. So working together, we trapped villagers, axolotls, sheep, a few cows . . ."

"AND I JUST TRAPPED ONE VERY AGGRESSIVE LLAMA," Ash said as she came running into the cavern.

Morgan appeared next. He entered the cavern at full speed, and he didn't stop. Mist swirled all around him. "The spider's on my tail!" he cried. "And I think the Slowness just wore off!"

Morgan was right. The spider appeared mere seconds later, leaping into the cavern and hissing. Theo pulled a lever, and a set of doors swung closed. Now every tunnel was blocked with an iron door. **The spider was trapped.**

And the kids were trapped with it.

Chapter 14

HOW CAN YOU TELL SPIDERS HATE TO BE TRAPPED? BECAUSE THEY'RE ALWAYS CLIMBING THE WALLS!

Po selected a sword from his inventory. The spider was big and scary. Its fangs were sharp, and its skin looked hairy. But it was also alone, without its army of mobs to protect it. This finally felt like a fight they could win.

The real question was did they *want* to fight it?

"LET'S TRY TALKING FIRST," Theo insisted. "The Evoker King is inside that spider somewhere. Or at least, a part of him is . . ."

"What if it's the part of

him that wanted to destroy us?" asked Po. "I think I'll hold on to my sword, just in case."

The spider looked at Po's sword and hissed. It skittered onto the wall.

"Wait!" said Ash. **"WE COME IN PEACE."**

"Don't you recognize us?" asked Jodi, hoping to appeal to some part of her friend the Evoker King.

Theo said quickly, "What do you know about the Fault? Can you tell us more about it?"

Morgan raised an eyebrow at Theo's question, but any discussion about that would have to come later.

The spider didn't speak. But it didn't attack, either. **It skittered along the wall, retreating into the mist and shadows at the far corner of the cavern.**

"Don't let it get away," warned Morgan.

"It can't get far," said Harper.

"Well, let's keep our eyes on it anyway," said Ash, peering into the darkness.

They all moved forward together.

And none of them saw the spider's trap in time to avoid it.

"Hey!" said Jodi. **"I'M SINKING!"**

Po realized she was right. They were *all* sinking. What had happened to the floor?

"It's the pit!" said Theo. "The one we dug for our first plan. It's full of cobwebs!"

"Then . . . we're helpless!" said Morgan, pulling against the sticky stuff. "It will take forever to get out of this."

Po had his sword out, but his arm was caught up in the sticky web. He couldn't quite get enough movement out of his arm to effectively swing the weapon. Everyone was in the same predicament. Only Morgan seemed to have any real mobility.

"I can move one hand. Do we have shears to cut through it?" said Ash. "Harper?"

"We left our shears in a chest aboveground," Harper said. "We didn't think we'd need them. . . ."

And then Po saw the red eyes shining above them.

"Our original trap worked after all," he said. "I mean, it worked out great for the spider!"

"WE DON'T HAVE ANY CHOICE," said Morgan. He took a bow from his inventory. "We're sitting ducks. We have to destroy the spider before it destroys us."

As if responding to Morgan's threat, the spider showed its fangs and hissed. Soupy green mist rolled down into the pit, making everything hazy.

"THAT WON'T SAVE YOU," said Morgan. He took aim with his bow. "And none of your friends can help you now, either."

Friends. The word triggered something in Po. Visions of mobs danced through his head: villagers and bunnies, llamas and sheep.

"Wait!" he cried. **"MORGAN, DON'T HURT IT."**

Morgan gave Po a strange look. But he lowered his bow. "Why not?" he asked.

"I think . . . I think I know what it wants," said Po. "It isn't attacking us. See? We're helpless, and it's only spitting that gas at us."

"Which is pretty rude!" said Jodi.

"Maybe." Po shrugged. "But the gas doesn't work on us. It only works on mobs. And it doesn't hurt mobs, right?"

"Right," said Ash. She smiled with understanding. "The gas makes mobs into its friends!"

"You mean . . ." Theo rubbed his blocky chin. "The spider is trying to *befriend* us right now?"

"IT'S A GOOD THEORY," said Harper. **"BUT HOW DO WE TEST IT?"**

"By extending our hands in friendship," said Po, trying to sound like the politicians he'd heard on TV. He turned his face up toward the spider. "Um, hello? **TERROR-ANTULA?** Is it okay if I call you that?"

The spider hissed.

"Yeah, okay, bad idea," said Po. "I just wanted to let you know that I understand where you're

coming from. It feels nice to surround yourself with friends. It feels really good to be popular."

The spider tilted its head. It seemed to be listening.

"ME? I LOVE BEING POPULAR," Po continued. "Being the center of attention is the best. But . . . I would never mind-zap anybody into following me around or force them to do what I wanted." He thought about Morgan's cookies and Jodi's refusal to spy for him. "Well, maybe I *have* tried to force people to do stuff. But that was wrong, and I regret it." He felt his friends' eyes on him, and he got a little nervous. But when he looked back, they were all smiling at him. There was no judgment in their eyes, only encouragement.

Po felt a new surge of confidence.

"THE ENDERMONSTER WAS THE PART OF THE EVOKER KING that was afraid to be seen," he said. "I think you're the opposite. You're the part of him that desperately wants friends. I think that's why you surround yourself with villagers and bunnies and any other mob you can find." Po shook his head sadly. **"BUT FORCING THEM . . .**

MANIPULATING THEM . . . CONTROLLING THEM? That's the wrong way to do it. You have to be honest, and open, and let your friends *choose* you." He smiled. "And we will choose you. We *want* to be your friends. I mean, you're kind of, sort of the Evoker King—which means we're kind of, sort of friends *already*."

The spider stood totally still, as if it was thinking about what Po had said.
Po wondered if he should say or do more. But then, after a long pause, the spider nodded, just once. The mob then erupted in a burst of light, pixels . . . and digital butterflies.

The butterflies swarmed over Po's head, briefly blocking his view. As the butterflies flew off, the

eeric green mist dissipated. Gone, too, was the
spider. In its place . . . was a long, blocky leg.

Po recognized it as the second leg of the Evoker
King. He whooped for joy, and the others echoed
his cry of excitement.

**They were one step closer to putting
their friend back together.**

Or they would be . . . just as soon as they were
able to cut themselves out of the massive tangle of
cobwebs.

Chapter 15

THE BIG DEBATE! THE MOMENT OF TRUTH! . . . AND THE REASON GYM IS CANCELED TODAY!

Po LIKED TO WIN. Often, that was a good quality. When he was on the basketball court . . . or rehearsing for a play . . . or studying for a test? That drive to succeed was hugely important.

But it was possible to be too competitive. To take things too far. To put just winning ahead of how you win.

He tried to remember that as he adjusted his microphone in the moments before his debate with Shelly Silver. The entire class had packed into the cafeteria to witness it. And Po found himself craving their applause.

But he reminded himself that he wasn't here

for applause. He was here to discuss important subjects that his fellow students cared deeply about. And he needed to take that seriously.

Mr. Malory stepped to the center of the stage and addressed the assembled students. "Greetings, Woodsword," he said. "As a neutral party, I've been asked to moderate this debate over my lunch hour. **Normally I'd be sad to miss lunch** . . . but I was going to eat a bologna sandwich today, so I'd rather be here with all of you."

Mr. Malory paused, as if waiting for laughter. But no one made a sound. He turned to Po and Shelly. **"Tough crowd,"** he whispered to them.

Shelly was at her own lectern, which was set up a few feet away from Po's. She didn't look nervous. In fact, she looked eager to begin.

"Let's start with you, Shelly," said Mr. Malory.

"Why do you want to be class president?"

Shelly didn't hesitate. **"I want to make a difference at Woodsword,"** she answered. "I want to help make our school the very best it can be. I have a plan to expand our after-school activities by twenty percent, and to reduce our carbon footprint by twice that percentage. That's why I gave out reusable spoons when I announced my campaign—the disposable plasticware that the cafeteria provides us is wasteful and unnecessary, and it has to go."

Po was stunned. It hadn't even occurred to him that her handouts were part of a waste-reduction plan. He'd thought she was just trying to be flashy!

"And I had to stay up late doing the math, but . . . **I think I may have a solution to the block party dilemma,**" said Shelly. "If we change the event into a ticketed fundraiser, we have the opportunity to keep the party fun . . . while actually *making* money instead of spending it. I think that might satisfy everybody!"

The students all applauded for Shelly, and Po found he couldn't blame them. He almost wanted to join them!

"Same question for you, Po," said Mr. Malory. **"Why do you want to be president?"**

Po thought for a moment about his answer. And he decided to be honest.

"I *don't* really want to be president," he said. He heard gasps from the crowd, but he didn't let that stop him. "What I *want* is to win the election, because winning feels good. And winning a *vote* makes you feel like people really like you." He sighed. "I like being the center of attention. But that's the *only* thing I would like about being president. I'm not actually ready for the responsibility. I mean, nobody told me there'd be *math* involved." He grinned. "And that's why . . . I've decided to endorse Shelly Silver for class president."

Now Shelly herself gasped. Everyone else seemed to be stunned into silence. Po looked into the crowd and saw that every student was sitting absolutely frozen in place.

Then he saw Morgan begin to clap.

And Jodi. And Harper and Theo and Ricky.

And then everybody else.

A huge cacophony of cheering and applause swept over Po like a wave. It was so loud that it almost felt like it could knock him backward.

He soaked it in. Being the center of attention really *did* feel good.

Especially when you were getting attention . . . for making the right choice.

He nodded to Shelly, then rolled away from the lectern.

Chapter 16

THE RESULTS ARE IN! EVERYBODY'S A WINNER! BUT THERE'S STILL ONE LITTLE PROBLEM. . . .

Jodi swung a pickaxe, and the "Vote for Po" sign was destroyed.

Po laughed. **"THAT LOOKED LIKE FUN."**

"It really was!" said Jodi, smiling.

Po and his friends had returned to the caverns of Minecraft. Back at school, the votes were in. Shelly had won by a landslide . . . and Po could not have been happier about that.

Woodsword's students had chosen the right candidate for the job.

It wasn't totally necessary to remove the glowing signs he'd placed throughout the caves. It wasn't as if anybody but the five of them would ever see them. But Po hoped that getting rid of the signs would help them put the whole experience behind them.

Especially the parts where he'd behaved badly.

The sooner they forgot about all that, the better he'd feel.

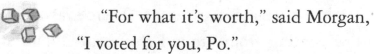

"For what it's worth," said Morgan, "I voted for you, Po."

"You did?" Po couldn't help it: he smiled.

"I think we all did," said Jodi, and Harper nodded.

"NOT BECAUSE YOU'RE OUR FRIEND," said Harper. **"BUT BECAUSE WE BELIEVE IN YOU."**

"You would have been a great president, Po," said Morgan. "Even if you weren't totally prepared . . . **YOU ALWAYS RISE TO MEET WHATEVER CHALLENGE YOU'RE FACED WITH.**"

"Aw, you guys," Po said dramatically. "Careful, or my high-tech VR goggles are gonna end up full of salt water."

As Morgan demolished another sign, Jodi reached down into a pond where a blue axolotl was swimming. **"I'M JUST GLAD EVERYTHING'S BACK TO NORMAL,"** she said, patting the mob's head with affection.

With the last sign taken down, the five friends prepared to return to the surface. But Theo pointed into the darkness. "What's that?" he asked.

Po saw what Theo meant. There was a faint glow coming from around the corner. "Did we miss one of the signs?" he asked.

But when he turned the corner, **he was met with a shock.**

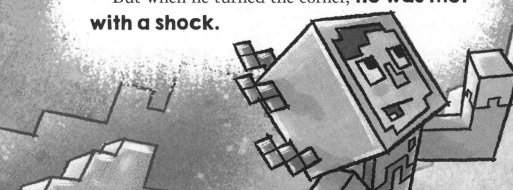

Big, blocky letters were shining on the cavern wall. Someone had written a message in glowing ink.

Po read the message out loud: "Come to the zoo . . . **if you dare.**"

"What does it mean?" asked Harper.

"Who could have written it?" asked Theo.

"We'll have to find out somehow," said Morgan.

"I hope we can pet the animals!" said Jodi.

Beneath the words was the image of a butterfly. **But somehow, that was not very comforting. . . .**

MINECRAFT is a game about placing blocks and going on adventures. Build, play, and explore across infinitely generated worlds of mountains, caverns, oceans, jungles, and deserts. Defeat hordes of zombies, bake the cake of your dreams, venture to new dimensions, or build a skyscraper. What you do in Minecraft is up to you.

Nick Eliopulos is a writer who lives in Brooklyn (as many writers do). He likes to spend half his free time reading and the other half gaming. He cowrote the Adventurers Guild series with his best friend and works as a narrative designer for a small video game studio. After all these years, endermen still give him the creeps.

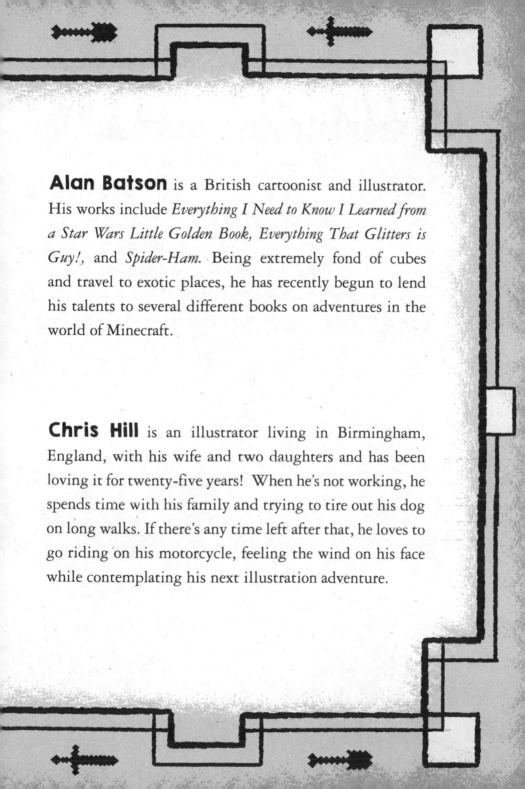

Alan Batson is a British cartoonist and illustrator. His works include *Everything I Need to Know I Learned from a Star Wars Little Golden Book, Everything That Glitters is Guy!,* and *Spider-Ham.* Being extremely fond of cubes and travel to exotic places, he has recently begun to lend his talents to several different books on adventures in the world of Minecraft.

Chris Hill is an illustrator living in Birmingham, England, with his wife and two daughters and has been loving it for twenty-five years! When he's not working, he spends time with his family and trying to tire out his dog on long walks. If there's any time left after that, he loves to go riding on his motorcycle, feeling the wind on his face while contemplating his next illustration adventure.

FROM BLOCKS TO PANELS,

MINECRAFT™

COMES TO COMICS

MINECRAFT: WITHER WITHOUT YOU VOLUME 1

After an intense battle with an enchanted Wither, Cahira and Orion's mentor is eaten and they are now alone! The two monster hunters go on a mission to get their mentor back, and meet an unlikely ally along the way!

978-1-50670-835-5 • $10.99 US/$14.99 CA
88 Pages Trade Paperback

MINECRAFT: WITHER WITHOUT YOU VOLUME 2

After saving their mentor from the belly of a Wither, twin monster hunters turn their sights on solving the mystery of their new friend's curse and set off a chain of events leading to the zombie apocalypse!

978-1-50671-886-6 • $10.99 US/$14.99 CA
88 Pages Trade Paperback

MINECRAFT

Tyler's family has to move but thankfully, he has a strong group of friends forever linked in the world of *Minecraft*! They go on the ultimate quest and face off against the Ender Dragon!

978-1-50670-834-8 • $10.99 US/$14.99 CA
88 Pages Trade Paperback

MINECRAFT VOLUME 2

When Evan and the gang find themselves assaulted by pirates, and then by an even bigger threat, all the players realize they must learn to rely on each other to overcome adversity.

978-1-506780-836-2 • $10.99 US/$14.99 CA
88 Pages Trade Paperback

MINECRAFT VOLUME 3

Candace, Evan, Grace, Tobi, and Tyler continue their adventures in the world of *Minecraft* and find themselves stumbling upon a mysterious ruined portal. Arriving to a strange and wonderful corner of the Nether that they've never seen, the group turn to their Nether expert, Grace, for help.

978-1-50672-580-2 • $10.99 US/$14.99 CA
88 Pages Trade Paperback

MINECRAFT: STORIES FROM THE OVERWORLD

With tales of rivals finding common ground and valiant heroes new (or not!) to the Overworld, this collection brings together stories from all realms, leaving no block unturned!

978-1-50670-833-1 • $14.99 US/$19.99 CA
88 Pages Hardcover

Minecraft.net
DarkHorse.com

MOJANG STUDIOS

DARK HORSE BOOKS